Shannon's Backyard

The Timmy

Book Eighteen

Story by Charles J LaBelle

Illustration by Jake Stories Publishing

Jake Stories Publishing
Children's stories and Jake Brain Training Games
www.jakestories.com

Jake Stories Publishing
Jake Brain Training Games
© 2016 Charles J. LaBelle

National Library Archives of Canada,
Cataloguing in Publishing Data
LaBelle, Charles J.
Shannon's Backyard
The Timmy
Book Eighteen
First Edition 2016
Jake Stories Publishing
Illustration by Jake Stories Publishing
ISBN 978-1-896710-90-7

Shannon ran down the path.

She was on her way to visit Mr. Tiller, Big Eyes the cat,

Chinook the horse and Itchy the flea.

She had three Shrinking-bush leaves tucked in her pocket.

She thought,

You must always be prepared.

You never know when you might have to shrink.

Bark! Bark! Bark!

Shannon jumped. She couldn't believe her eyes.

She said, "Well, hello good looking!

What are you doing on Mr. Tiller's path?

Are you going to see Big Eyes?"

A small, fluffy light golden dog blocked Shannon's path.

He just sat there and barked.

Shannon knelt down and put her head against the dog's.
Now we can Thought-talk! You can tell me what the problem is.

The dog thought, *My name is Timmy.*
I'm Itchy the flea's friend.
I know he went to Mr. Tiller's on Chinook, the big black horse.
Can you help me find him?

Shannon answered, *I sure can! I'm going to visit him.*
Do you want to come with me?

Timmy said, *Oh, yes! Please!*
I have Itchy's father and mother with me. They are very worried.

Itchy's brother and sister, Hop and Jump, have run away to join the circus!
Itchy is the only one they'll listen to. Mom and Dad flea want Itchy and me to
bring the children back from Tillerville.
They're preforming at the Fish Food restaurant.

Shannon thought,
Mr. Tiller can Thought-talk to all the critters without touching heads.
We can get everyone's advice. He can tell me what everyone thinks.

Shannon suggested, *After we get some ideas, we can make a plan to bring them back home.*

Timmy answered, *I hope we can. I'm a very special dog.*
My fur is home to Itchy's family! I love my fleas!
They share my food and never bite me.
We tell each other stories and play together. I watch them do gymnastic tricks.
They're amazing! Itchy used to live in my warm fur. Things change!
He said he wanted to live on Chinook because he runs faster.
Itchy taught me and his brother, Hop, and sister, Jump, circus tricks.
He always liked excitement.
You should see him perform on the trapeze.

Shannon thought, *I think I can help! Let's hurry to Mr. Tiller's.*
Shannon and Timmy trotted down the path.

Shannon sang,
♫*We're on our way, on this sunny day, to solve another problem.*
Timmy and I will find a way to make big ones look like small ones.
A dog who likes fleas is hard to find, and I'm very glad I've met one.
He's very concerned about his friends, even though they're tiny small ones. ♫

Shannon and Timmy ran into Mr. Tiller's garden, all out of breath.

Mr. Tiller was weeding his carrot patch.

Chinook was lying in the grass with Big Eyes sleeping beside him.

Itchy was sitting on Chinook's ear.

Shannon called, "Mr. Tiller! Mr. Tiller! Mr. Tiller! We have a problem!"

Timmy joined in,

Bark! Bark! Bark!

Everyone jumped.

Mr. Tiller dropped his hoe and shouted,

Chinook jumped up on his back legs and called,

Big Eyes jumped into the air.

Her hair stood straight out. Her eyes got big.

She screeched, **Meow!**

Shannon said, "Sorry, guys. We didn't mean to startle you."

Mr. Tiller laughed and said,

"Shannon! You know how to make us jump."

Mr. Tiller continued, "I'm glad to see you. Who's your new friend?
What's going on?"

Shannon said, "This is Timmy.
All of Itchy's family used to live in his nice warm fur. Things changed!
Itchy went to live on Chinook.
Today, Itchy's brother and sister,
Hop and Jump, ran off to join the circus.
Itchy's mom and dad are very worried.
Will you Thought-talk with them?
You can listen to their ideas and tell me what they say.
We can work together and make a plan to help.

Please, Mr. Tiller! Please Mr. Tiller! Can we do that right now?"

Mr. Tiller answered,
"Oh, Shannon you always ask so nicely, the only thing I can say is, yes.
But we must have Itchy join in this conversation.
I think he'll be part of the solution to the problem.

Shannon said, "Oh yes! We'll include everyone's ideas, including
Chinook's, Big Eyes' and Timmy's. They'll have lots of good suggestions.
Hooray! We'll have a conference and solve the problem."

Everyone sat in a circle and Thought-talked with Mr. Tiller.
He told Shannon all the critters suggestions.

Mom and Dad flea stood on Timmy's ears and said,
It's okay to have fun but children must come home before it gets dark.

Itchy stood on Chinook's ear and said,
They're nearly grown-up fleas and they need to have more freedom.

Chinook said,
It would be good to see their flea circus performance before I offer advice.

Big Eyes said,
Yes, let's go to the Fish Food restaurant.
We can meet Itchy's brother and sister.

Shannon said, "I agree. How should we travel to Tillerville?"

Mr. Tiller suggested, "Timmy and Big Eyes can run."

Shannon said, "Mr. Tiller and I can ride on Chinook, and Itchy can sit on
his ear. Is that okay with you Chinook?"

Whinny !

"That's yes in horse language," said Shannon.

Mr. Tiller added,

"Chinook says, *Okay, as long as Itchy promises to stay out of my ear.*
I'm getting thoughts back saying *Yes* from Big Eyes and Timmy."

Shannon cheered,

"Hooray! Let's go! Last one at the Fish Food restaurant
has to buy cream soda floats, for everyone."

Mr. Tiller said, "I'm getting thoughts back from Big Eyes and Timmy.

They say **NO FAIR !** *Chinook can run faster and we don't use money.*

Shannon cheered, "Okay! I'll buy!"
Off they went,
galloping and running as fast as they could.

The group reached the Tillerville restaurant in record time.
They settled round a courtyard table in the small circus tent and waited.

Everyone was out of breath and needed to rest.
Shannon ordered: two saucers full of cream soda floats,
one for Timmy and one for Big Eyes; five teaspoons full, one for each
member of Itchy's family; two big glasses filled to the top, for herself and
Mr. Tiller.

Shannon asked for a very special order for Chinook.

She said, "Give Chinook a full pail of cream soda float." But Shannon
didn't have enough money to buy a full pail.

The restaurant manager said,
"It's free for you Shannon. Enjoy the show!"

Sitting so close to the stage was exciting.

They could see the small performers waiting to come on the stage.

When the drinks came, the show started like magic.

The courtyard lights dimmed and the stage lights came on.

Out came twenty fleas.

Clap! Clap! Clap!

Some fleas walked a tight rope.

Clap! Clap! Clap!

Others dove off a platform into a dish of water.

Clap! Clap! Clap!

Suddenly the most exciting thing happened !

A girl flea and a boy flea climbed the ladder to the trapeze.
They jumped from the platforms and caught the bar.
They swung back and forth on the trapeze.
The girl flea let go.
She sailed through the air and started falling to the ground.

The crowd went

The boy flea reached out and tried to catch her.
Their hands touched.
He snatched her hand and swung her back to the platform.

 Everyone cheered.

Itchy shouted in flea talk and Mr. Tiller translated,
"Wow! That's their miss-em catch-em act!
That's my brother and sister, Hop and Jump"

Hop and Jump kept everyone on the edge of their seats.
Their show lasted for twenty minutes.

After the end of the show, Itchy went backstage to tell Jump and Hop to join them for cream soda floats.

Sad.... Sad.... Sad

Itchy came back to the table.
He looked very sad.
His chin was tucked into his chest and his eyes were full of flea tears.

Mr. Tiller translated.
"Hop and Jump are afraid to come and sit with us.
They said if they try to leave the stage the flea circus manager will have the
Strongman grab them and lock them in a room."

Shannon jumped to her feet.
She shouted,
"He can't do that! The big bully! He'll have to talk to me, right now.
Oh dear! I'll have to shrink to Thought-talk to him.
Well, here goes!
Excuse me while I stand on the table and shrink to three inches tall.
I'll still be much bigger than the flea Strongman.
Watch this!
We'll see who can be the strongest man! - err lady! - err girl!"

Shannon took the three Shrinking-bush leaves from her pocket.
She said, "No pricking my finger this time.
I don't have to put blood on the leaves to be three inches tall.
Watch this! I close my eyes and spin around ten times to the right.
Stop . . . Wave my arms above my head.
Stop . . . Turn ten times to the left.
Stop . . . Put my hands above my head and count to ten.
I shrink while I count to ten.
One, two, three, four, five, six, seven, eight, nine, ten."

"Now you better watch out, Mr. Strongman!
Here I come!"
Shannon jumped off the table onto the stage.
She ran behind the curtain.
Strongman was dragging Hop and Jump.
He pulled them by the back of the neck.
He walked towards a dark room at the back of the stage.

Shannon shouted,
"Stop where you are! Leave those children alone, you big bully!"

Strongman stopped and shouted,

Hiss . . . squeek . . .clack, clack !

In flea talk that means, "*Who's going to make me?*"

Timmy shoved his nose through the curtain.

Strongman dropped Hop and Jump and ran!

He screamed so hard that he spit out his false teeth.

They hit the floor, clattered, bounced twice, and settled into a corner.

Strongman dived into the dark room and slammed the door.

Strongman was afraid.
Sweat ran down his head into his eyes.
He couldn't see where his teeth were.

He thought,
I'll hide in here forever if I have to!

Shannon, Hop, and Jump climbed on Timmy's back
for a ride back to the table.

They sang as they went.

♩ *That bully Strongman was really mean,*
until Timmy growled and made him scream.
His legs were shaking, his knees were weak.
We couldn't even hear him squeak.

He lost his teeth on the stage floor.
Now he can't bite us anymore.
Into his dark room he ran.
That nasty, mean, cruel old man.

Hooray! Hooray! for Timmy.
Timmy saved the day.
Strongman won't dare come out, till we have gone away.
Hooray! Hooray! for Timmy.
Timmy saved the day. ♫

Shannon threw the shrinking-bush leaves into the air and grew to normal size.

Everyone sat down in front of their cream soda floats. The manager gave everyone special cookie treats and apologized for the mean, bully behavior of the Strongman flea.

Shannon stood up and said, "Thank you Mr. Manager.
Then she sat down and everyone cheered,
"The manager is kinder now!"

Shannon sang,
♫*Hooray! Hooray! The gang's all here.*
We're going to drink our cream soda floats,
and relax a while, before we go.
Hooray! Hooray! The gang's all here.
We're all together now.
We're having our cream soda floats.
The manager gave Chinook a bag of oats.
Hooray! Hooray! The gang's all here.
We've had a big adventure and we're all together now.♫

www.ingramcontent.com/pod-product-compliance
Lightning Source LLC
Chambersburg PA
CBHW041541240626
47164CB00002B/86